FROM THE OZARK MOUNTAINS

TALES OF

PEE POT POLLIES

AND PAPER DOLLIES

Jo Hammers

Paranormal Crossroads & Publishing

Pee Pot Polly

Art work by Jo Hammers, 2012.

Table of Contents

FROM THE OZARK MOUNTAINS

TALES OF

PEE POT POLLIES

AND PAPER DOLLIES

Jo Hammers
Paranormal Crossroads & Publishing

CHAPTER ONE

Eddie Meets Pee Pot Polly

P ee Pot Polly was my doll who wet after feeding her. She would hold her water as long as you kept her on her back. When you turned her upright, all the liquid in her would come gushing out.

Eddie was my playmate next door. He liked to play with me, but he hated my dolls. He would tear their arms off, or throw them like footballs. I told my poor dollies that someday, I would get even with him. Pee Pot Polly was my secret weapon.

Eddie was delighted when I called him on the phone and asked him to come over and play house. I gave Polly her bottle of water before he arrived, and left her diaper off. I had her lying so nice and peaceful on her back in the doll bed. After we played a few minutes, I pretended that Polly was crying.

"Eddie, will you pick her up?" I asked.

It was wonderful revenge. She wet all down the front of his shirt.

He yelled, "Yuk!"

I laughed so hard that there were tears in my eyes. Insulted and crying, having been peed on, Eddie went home. I had one less friend for awhile.

CHAPTER TWO

Sweet Revenge

Annie was my best friend. The only problem we had was that her dolls were always a little bit better than mine. She had, in her opinion, a better and more expensive version of my Pee Pot Polly. To hear her tell it, her doll was superior and could pee the most. Annie always had to be the best. I was determined that my doll was going to outdo her doll if it killed me. I was tired of always being made to feel second best. I had a plan and called Annie on the phone and invited her over to play house just as I had Eddie.

On that particular occasion, I prepared a thin mixture of mustard and water. I fed Polly and prepared for sweet revenge. I pulled the same trick on Annie that I did on Eddie. When she went to pick up my naked Pee Pot Polly doll, the thin mustard mixture squirted all down the front of her new white dress. Mother was not happy with me. However, I was all smiles. My Pee Pot Polly could do something that hers could not. Annie went home in tears, and I had two less friends for awhile.

CHAPTER THREE

Uncle George

Uncle George was also on my list. He always made insinuations, when he visited, that I smelled like my dog. He would then state that he did not like dogs. I got what he meant, even if he didn't come right out and say it. I didn't care for him either.

The weekend arrived and he came for his routine Saturday visit with my mother. I was prepared for him, just as I had been for Eddie and Annie.

My mother had a cheap bottle of perfume

sitting on her dresser that someone had given her for Christmas. I asked her for the bottle, stating I wanted to dump the perfume out and use the glass vial to put flowers in when I set my toy tea set up.

"You may have it. However, I want you to go out by the alley and dump it out and be careful not to get any of the smelly stuff on you. Wash the bottle out with the garden hose. I don't want any of that cheap smell in my house." She stated as she stood washing dishes at the kitchen sink. "Don't tell your Aunt Jean I gave it to you."

"Thank you mother . . . I will be careful with the smell and wash the bottle out." I said politely grinning on the inside.

In the bathroom, I dumped the cheap perfume in my doll bottle. Pee Pot Polly was a good baby. She drank the whole bottle of Aunt Jean's gift of cheap dime store perfume. Boy did the stuff stink.

I lay Peep Pot Polly carefully flat on the living room floor awaiting Uncle George's arrival.

A knock sounded at the front door. I recognized the knock. It was Uncle George. I knew he would be wearing his usual suit and necktie. Uncle George was a salesman and prided himself in how he looked.

"What is that smell?" He asked entering and sitting down in our living room's best chair.

"It sort of smells like a dead mouse!" My mother added as she scrunched her nose and sniffed.

I did not reply. I put on my angel face and pretended to look under the skirt of the couch for a dead mouse.

"Your dog has probably got behind your couch and done his business." Uncle George stated rolling his eyes.

"I will pull the couch out and look after you leave." My mother replied. She then exited to fix refreshments.

I abandoned my search for dead mice and put on my best fake smile. Mother said ladies always smiled no matter what. I had my fake smile mastered thanks to her.

My mother made a couple comments on the weather in a loud voice from the kitchen. Uncle George wrinkled up his nose and didn't answer. He seemed really annoyed with the smell.

My mother and Uncle George always enjoyed a cup of hot tea and cookies together on Saturdays. He was a tea sipping Saturday nuisance in my book.

However, today was different. I was making the most of his visit and getting sweet revenge for him insinuating that I smelled like a dog on his previous visit.

I picked up my naked Pee Pot Polly Doll and carefully held her flat pretending to scold her for crying. Then I asked Uncle George to hold Pee Pot Polly while I ran to help mother with the tea and cookies. He agreed. I lay Pee Pot Polly flat on his knees and then made a dash for the kitchen knowing he would upright her and discard her with me gone from the room.

I was right! Unrepeatable words were instantly being shouted in the living room.

I tried not to giggle as I pulled cookies from a bag and placed them on a little serving dish. I was trying to act like a helpful angel to my mother. Shocking, profane words from Uncle George's mouth suddenly floated into the kitchen.

My mother, being a little Victorian in her thinking, was outraged at the profanity. I could see it on her face. Profanity was a no-no in her book and she definitely didn't want me hearing it. She abandoned me, the tea, and cookies to see what was wrong.

"Whew! What is it?" He yelled in a disgusted, gasping voice to her, when she entered the living room.

I then heard some more foul language that was best not heard by a young angel like me. I put on my best smiling angel face. I knew that he now smelled worse than my dog; possibly even a skunk.

Mother was furious! Uncle George left without having tea and cookies. In my book, it was worth it. However, my backside got blistered. There were no laws back then about not spanking a child. I got the full hand treatment and then stood in a corner. It was all worth it.

After that incident, Pee Pot Polly took a mysterious vacation and never came back. Mother got over being mad, but never bought me another doll that wet. Pee Pot Polly had been a true friend and had taken the heat for me and then disappeared.

Uncle George, however, was on the hot seat. He had a hard time explaining to my Aunt Margaret why he reeked with the smell of cheap perfume. She slipped around and asked me if I had put perfume in my doll bottle like Uncle George had told her. Of course, being the angel I am, I told her no and asked her what she was talking about. I then took her to my bedroom and showed her a little blue heart bottle of Blue Waltz toilet water. I told her that was the only perfume that I owned. She took the lid off and smelled it. I could tell by the look on her face that the perfume she smelled on Uncle George was not mine. Did I tell you that Uncle George had a mysterious black eye the next Saturday when he came to call? I overheard my mother ask him if Aunt Margaret did it.

I will always miss Pee Pot Polly. We were good together.

CHAPTER FOUR

Making Mud Pies

One of my delights, back in the 1940's (during World War II) and in the early 1950's, was making mud pies in the summertime. Some of the poorer class of the United States were just getting their lives put back together. My mother had one pot and one skillet to cook in. We ate meat once a week and had dessert once a week. The dessert was usually apple pie because we had a tree behind the house. When there was money for the ingredients, banana crème pies with toasted brown meringue on top were baked. My mother was a pie maker.

A child imitates the environment around them. In the summer, in my pretend kitchen, I made mud chocolate, meringue pies. My pies had to be chocolate because the mud was brown. I would dig up some dirt, add water, and then pour my mixture out into whatever I could come up with that looked like a tiny round pie pan. My mother rarely made cobbler or what we call now, sheet cake. She made pies and layer cakes. I did the same in my summer kitchen which was a short board stretched across two rocks.

Toy pots and pans were hard to come up with. Sometimes you used the caps and lids off of a fruit jar, or a tuna or sardines can. Nothing was thrown away back then at our house.

My parents feared the depression would return and they might need what little they had to survive. My mother had two dresses back then and one pair of shoes. My father had cardboard inside of his work boots because the soles were worn out. Toy dishes for me were not a priority. I was not the only little girl in the neighborhood making do. Times were what they were.

On the particular day I remember, it was very hot and my mud pies had dried (baked) quickly in the hot sun. I turned them out of their jar cap pie pans and was marveling at how perfect they were just like my mothers. They were perfect till my little brother popped over to my kitchen to take a look.

"What are they?" He asked looking at my little, dried, round, molded, dirt concoctions.

"Chocolate Pie, "I replied with pride.

"They don't look like chocolate pie to me. Chocolate pie has meringue on top. You will never be the pie maker mom is. Everyone knows chocolate pie has to have meringue on top."

I remember biting my lip. "We are in a depression and I don't have anything to make meringue out of!" I retorted.

"What is that white stuff you have on the side of your face?" He then asked.

"It's that new, awful tasting white toothpaste that mom bought." I replied wiping the side of my face.

He then walked away to pursue his own play goals.

A light bulb went on in my head.

I wiped my muddy hands on the grass and headed for the house, peeping to see where my mother was and what she was up to. Then I slipped into the toiletries cabinet and took the tube of white toothpaste. I had discovered a way to put meringue on my mud pies.

Returning outside, I took off the little cap and began to squirt the white goo all over the top of my beautiful mud chocolate pies.

About that time, my friend Sharon, from next door, walked over to see what I was up to.

"Wow . . . they look real!" She exclaimed. Then her mother discovered she was out of her yard and yelled for her. She immediately ran home.

I was really pleased. I was a pie baker like my mother.

However, my glory was short lived. I heard a stern voice half shouting behind me. "Barbara Jo . . . !"

That ended my career as a summer time, mud pie baker.

EAT YOUR SOUP

~ *A Poem*

Come on dolly and eat your soup!

I have cooked all day just for you.

Soup and crackers will calm your tummy

And friends like me will make you feel sunny.

I could give your soup to the cat.

I just do not know where he is at.

Back yard birdie could eat your crackers.

Please try to eat a little faster.

Do you hear mother calling?

I must go so please quit stalling.

I know you are not feeling well.

You will get better and not look so pale.

Come on Dolly and eat your soup.

CHAPTER FIVE

Rag Dolls

Mothers back in the depression era had to get creative when there was no money for toys and Christmas was around the corner. It seemed frivolous to spend money on dolls when your child had holes in her shoes. So, mothers who could sew made rag dolls with elaborate wardrobes from scraps of worn out clothing. Finding stuffing for the dolls was the problem. If you stuffed them with scraps, they were lumpy. Stuffing a doll with feathers from old pillows was equally as bad; not to mention stuffing them with dried beans. If you washed a bean stuffed doll, you had bean soup.

My friend's father worked at a saw mill. Her Christmas dolls always smelled like sawdust. That was good if the sawdust was cedar. The dolls had a very interesting perfume and kept the moths away. I recall her having one doll that we named Cedarella whom we thought would never catch a fella because she smelled. She was a real smelly mess after we tried to cure her problem. We slipped out her mother's vanilla and doused her. That didn't work, so we powder puffed her with Talcum. Our efforts only made her worse and my friend's mother declared her to be a front porch only doll. My friend's dog vacated the front porch and became a back porch dog. However, we didn't abandon Cedarella who smelled so bad she couldn't catch a fella. Our last attempt to cure her problem was with bleach. We poured half a jug of bleach in a pan, not realizing you were supposed to dilute it. We dropped her in, left her there, and went about our business forgetting her till the next day. When we returned, the bleach had eaten holes in Cedarella. She had drowned or bleach fish had eaten her. We fished her out and gave her a proper burial in the back behind the wood shed. We found a rock and wrote on it, HERE LIES CEDARELLA WHO NEVER HAD A CHANCE TO CATCH A FELLA. She was eaten by fish.

CEDARELLA

THE RAG DOLL

~ *A Poem*

There are many dolls in my little girl's room.

Breakable dolls sit on high shelves.

They are so lonely.

Plastic dollies are carelessly tossed about.

Neglect is evident.

Paper dolls sleep in cardboard boxes.

The dark must be very frightening!

I am a special doll and have a place upon the bed.

The little girl's mother made me from scraps.

I wear handmade fabric dresses.

I am a gift of love! I am a gift of Love!

Every night, I fall asleep in the arms of an angel.

CHAPTER SIX

Marie's Love Story

Marie was in love with Melvin and it was Christmas time about the year of 1929 or 1930. Girls got married earlier back then. She was fifteen and he was twenty. Marie and her sisters waited for their beaus, as they called them, to arrive for Christmas Eve bearing gifts. Marie had two presents for Melvin. They were wrapped and waiting. She had purchased for him a pair of gloves and a necktie.

Marie had two older sisters who also had beaus and the y loved to give her advice on the proper way to handle different situations concerning courting. On this Christmas occasion, they told Marie to give her beau, Melvin, only one gift if he brought her one gift. If he brought her nothing, then give him only one gift and then cry when he gave her nothing to shame him.

The three sisters were decked out in their Christmas best waiting for their beaus.

Marie's arrived first. Melvin knocked on the door. Marie's sisters quickly took position behind her peeping and snooping to see whether Melvin had brought her a gift. When Marie opened the door, she and her sisters were shocked to see how many gifts he had brought her.

"May I come in?" Melvin asked from behind a stack of packages rising clear to his chin.

Melvin had spent his whole paycheck for the week on Marie. He bought her a scarf, gloves, handkerchiefs, a vanity set, candy, and several other items. They were all wrapped nicely and he was grinning. Marie gave him both of her presents grinning herself.

Shortly after Melvin arrived, Marie's two older sister's beaus came for Christmas Eve bringing each of them one gift. The two older sisters were not particularly impressed with their beaus' offerings.

Melvin and Marie were my parents. My mother loved to tell that story at Christmas time.

CHAPTER SEVEN

Poopsie & Boopsie

Poopsie and Boopsie stood on a shelf at the fall carnival. Forty other dolls stood with them. All looked pretty similar. They were carnival dolls, prizes to be given away to lucky winners of a Carnival booth game. They were made of a chalk like substance and were very fragile. Their clothes were painted on, but real feathers were attached to them on headbands.

Poopsie and Boopsie were best friends. They could not bear the thought of being separated. Ever since the day they had been born in a foreign factory, they had been best friends. They had been everywhere together on the Carnival Circuit. No one ever chose to take them home because they were rejects or flawed.

Some factory worker had given them a less than desirable makeup job with his paint. Boopsie had blue lips. One fingernail had not been painted on Poopsie. They were factory rejects, or seconds meant for discard. The carnival game booth owner just used them for filler on his shelf to make the other dolls look good.

Poopsie and Boopsie did not know they were less than desirable. There were no mirrors for them to look in. They saw themselves as having been, in the past, lucky. However, they feared that one day soon their luck would run out and they would be torn from each other's arms and be lost to each other forever. So, they clung to each other each time a winner picked a doll for a prize. Then, they sighed in relief when it was not one of them.

The last night of the Carnival season arrived. The number of dolls standing happily on the wooden shelves above the game was dwindling. Poopsie and Boopsie had watched in tears as their other doll friends left one by one with their new owners. Night shadows were falling. There were no electric lights in the booths back in their day. When night fell, the booths closed down. The two dolls prayed for the sun to drop behind the western horizon. If they made it to winter storage, they would be lucky once more.

Poopsie said, "Stand sloppy and pucker your blue lips. I will frown and show my white fingernail that has no polish. No one will want our uniqueness!"

"I will put my worst foot forward." Boopsie replied.

Nine dolls were on the shelf. A group of college boys with their sweethearts stopped at the booth and took turns playing the game. Their girlfriends squealed with delight as their beaus were winners. The Carnival prize dolls dwindled.

Poopsie counted, "Eight, seven, six, five, four, three, two . . . Thank God they are gone.

We are the only dolls left standing."

"That was a close one, Poopsie. Once more, we are lucky." Boopsie exclaimed with a sigh of relief.

Then a teen girl stepped up to the Carnival booth and tried to win the game. Poopsie and Boopsie clung to each other in desperation. They were the only dolls left. It looked like their time together as best friends was surely coming to an end. The two dolls trembled as they watched the girl play the game. Once more, they were lucky. She was not a winner.

Just as the sun was falling below the tree line in the west, a little girl about seven stepped up to the booth with her parents standing behind her. Poopsie and Boopsie were re-lieved when the father did not play the game. They stood a better chance of being lucky if the little girl played.

However, their lucky streak ended. The

little girl won. Both dolls burst into tears. Then they wondered which of them the little girl would choose.

"Which doll would you like?" The Carnival game owner asked.

The little girl eyed them. First she looked at Boopsie and then at Poopsie. Then she would repeat the process. She just could not decide. The keeper of the game booth was getting impatient. It was late, the sun had dropped below the horizon, and he was anxious to tear down his tent and game. The Carnival season was officially over. The little girl stood on one foot and then the other trying to decide.

Poopsie and Boopsie were in tears from the prolonged agony caused by the little girl's indecision. One of them would be spending the winter alone in a cardboard box in storage.

Finally, the game booth keeper, who was tired and annoyed with the child's indecision, said, "Guess what little girl? This is your lucky night. I am going to give you both dolls."

Poopsie and Boopsie could hardly believe their ears. They still could be best friends forever. They were lucky.

CHAPTER EIGHT

Paper Doll Valentines

There were no huge supermarkets when I was growing up. You purchased your groceries and other small items at little mom and pop corner grocery stores. They were small spaces about the size of some people's family rooms now-a-days. Every inch of their interior displayed something. Behind the counter of the one we did business with, the owner carried a few holiday items for the different seasons.

Between 1950 and 1954, my mom and pop store sold penny valentines. They were the

usual little treasures that kids exchanged at school. However, for a nickel you could buy a large valentine that had a little girl paper doll on it, as well as one set of clothes to punch out and dress her with. You were really a special little girl, if someone gave you one of those. Whole paper doll books could be purchased for ten to twenty-five cents.

I never received one of those treasured paper doll valentines, but I have pleasant memories of looking at them. Once, when my friend and I could not afford one of the little beauties for ourselves, we drew a paper doll valentine for each other and colored it with crayons. I wish I still had the little handmade valentine. Things, people take the time to make us, are far more valuable than those we purchase with a nickel that has no love put into it. My sister says her favorite paper doll was one that I drew for her when she was pre-elementary school age. It was drawn, cut out, and colored with crayons in the days when there was no money for toys. She still has it and it is at least fifty-five years old. It was drawn on a Big Chief lined tablet. My sister did not mind that the special paper doll had Big Chief tablet stripes running across her.

CHAPTER NINE

Time Out for Tea

My parents, who lived in the Ozark Mountains during the Great Depression, were not tea drinkers. They drank coffee. The only exception was the once a year digging of Sassafras root. It was boiled down and a red colored tea made from it. The brew was nasty, smelly stuff. My parents drank it for a couple of days as a spring thing, and then they returned to their coffee. It was sort of a yearly ritual.

Hot tea or iced tea was never made at our house. If we had visitors, men or women, they were offered coffee. Instead of prim and

proper tea parties, we had friends and family over for Coffee. There was not enough food in our depression day pantry, or that of our family and friends, to invite someone for dinner.

One of my favorite memories is of the times my uncle and aunt, from Kansas City, would drive two or so hours to return home to the Ozark Mountains. We were usually the first stop as they turned off the highway. Uncle Julian and Aunt Myrtle would arrive in two cars. The reason being, my uncle was a coon hunter. Riding with him in his car would be four to eight coon hounds, all riding like passengers. When he stopped in front of our house; he would get out, attach ropes to all the dogs' collars, and then secure them to my mother's three apple trees at the side of the house. To a little girl of six or seven, the huge hounds looked like monsters. They would bay, bark, and eye you as they panted and let their drooling tongues hang from their mouths. Aunt Myrtle would come with their four boys in a second car. That never changed.

My brothers would take our four boy cousins and head off to the back yard to play. I stayed in the house in fear of the dogs. I was a girl and not as adventurous as my brothers. Besides, I had big ears and loved to listen to what gossip was being shared. There were no televisions back at that time. Visitors and their stories were entertainment.

My uncle and aunt would immediately head for my mother's kitchen where they would seat themselves at her table. Mom would take an old fashioned aluminum coffee pot and boil down coffee grounds. When it was boiling hot, she would pour four cups. It wasn't unusual back then for the coffee to have some grounds in it. There were no paper filters back then. To go with the coffee, my mother would cut a freshly made apple pie and serve it. The fruit pastry was regularly served to company at our house because the apples were free. We had three mature apple trees during the Great Depression.

While eating pie and drinking coffee, my Uncle Julian would tell wild tales about coon hunting and buying and selling hounds. Aunt Myrtle preferred to discuss what was going on in the church she attended and her crochet projects. She always brought her projects with her to show off. She was a doily maker. After eating the pie and drinking the coffee, my uncle and father would excuse themselves and go out back to smoke and check out the coon hounds. Then my aunt and mother would go to the bedroom where my mother would show the quilt she was currently working on and discuss whatever secret female problems there were.

During the depression, there wasn't money to waste buying fabric for quilts. My mother recycled old clothing. I remember one really heavy quilt she made out of worn out jeans and work pants that my father and brothers could no longer wear. Once, she was given a brown paper bag of neckties. A neighbor man died and his wife didn't know what to do with them. She knew my mother cut up everything for quilt blocks. My mother made a neck tie quilt from the silk treasures.

There were no prim and proper, tea drinking ladies in big hats that dropped in at our house. What you would find were friends, family, and an occasional hobo knocking. It was not unusual for us to feed a hobo and my father to sit with him out back having coffee. As I said, there were not tea parties at our house. I am sure that the piece of apple pie was the one meal for the day for some of our visitors.

My mother had three brothers. Her oldest brother, Earl, was a fisherman. He would come for coffee about eight in the morning. My mother would have him a cup of coffee ready and a piece of pie. When he arrived, he would pull a stringer of fish from the trunk of his car and put them in a galvanized metal tub of water out front. My parents had an outside water faucet in front of the house. Then he would have coffee with my mother before going to work. My father hunted rabbits and squirrels for meat. My uncle caught fish. My mother cooked whatever came to her kitchen and shared what she had, apples.

My aunts didn't have money to spoil nieces with fancy dolls or toys. What they did was share their uniqueness or talents. Aunt Myrtle taught me how to crochet doll hats. Another aunt, named Golden, taught me how to crochet doll dresses. My mother's lady coffee guests were not prim and proper types. They possibly had two dresses and one pair of shoes. I had three dresses when growing up and that was because I went to school.

The third dress was a financial splurge for me. I wore one dress, had one in the laundry, and a clean one for the next day. My mother washed, ironed, and rotated the three dresses. My brothers had two pair of jeans each and three shirts. There was no waste or frivolous spending. When we outgrew our clothing, it was either passed down to younger siblings, or made its way to my mother's quilt scraps. I recall my mother making jean pot holders for her kitchen out of pants that were too worn or soiled to put into a quilt.

One summer, my Aunt Golden came to stay with us during the day for a week or so. She had been ill and couldn't be left alone, due to fainting spells. Uncle Buck would bring her each morning before he went to work and picked her up at the end of the day. She would sit on the back porch and crochet to pass the time. I watched her needle fly. Seeing I was interested, she taught me how to crochet dresses for my small doll. Gifts, except at Christmas, were rare. Before the two weeks was up, Aunt Golden gave me one of her treasured crochet needles and a spool of white crochet thread. It was a gift of love in a time when there was no money to buy gifts.

Making Snowmen

When elementary school let out for the Christmas Holidays in the early 1950s, my friends and I had one thing on our mind. We intended to play in the snow, have snow ball fights, and make snow men. We had been cooped up in school for almost four months. We were ready to be outside.

My brothers did most of the snow ball rolling and forming of our snowman's body and head. I patted snow on to cover flaws in the balls and give the snowman a smooth white look. Sometimes when you rolled balls for the body, you got dead leaves and dirt mixed in. I was assigned to pat snow on dirty spots. That was okay with me. I wanted a clean snow man.

My brothers and I were so excited that year

about being out of school. The first day of Christmas break, we wanted to stay out doors. Of course that was impossible. We had to return inside to warm ourselves and to eat. I recall taking in two snowballs I had made. They melted beside my plate as I ate my lunch, a peanut butter sandwich. Being a first grader, you just didn't understand why your snow balls had to go and melt on you. In exasperation, my mother told me to take my sandwich and the snowballs outside. She wasn't in the mood to clean up melting snowballs that were dripping off onto her kitchen floor. I saw eating outside that day as great fun. I saw myself as being invited to lunch by our snowman. I even shared my sandwich with our dog and cat.

Because I showed so much interest in our snowman, my mother made me a stuffed snowman out of a white feed sack for Christmas. I liked my man very much. No one in our neighborhood had a snowman rag doll.

Come
To
Tea !

TEA TIME

~ *A Poem*

At Tea Time, I invited Emily the cat.

She jumped on the table and that was that.

Next I invited Oscar my pet dog.

He drooled on my dishes and ate like a hog.

Last I invited my monstrous little brother.

He broke my dishes and I yelled for mother.

To Tea I will now invite only dollies and bears.

They have good manners and treat my things

With care!

By Jo Hammers

EMILY

TEA BISCUITS

TEA BAGS

Jo 2012

CHAPTER TEN

The Unconventional Winter Doll

Doll artists use all sorts of mediums to create dolls from. One of the most common substances is snow. All of us have made playful creatures from snow, never thinking we were making a plaything, or a doll. We have wrapped them and dressed them just like dolls or paper dolls. They are a short term, or disposable play thing. When they melt they are gone. However, Frosty lives on in our memories, just as conventional childhood dolls and paper dolls do.

Winter is fun and sometimes parents go to

extremes to make snowy day moments special for their children. Once upon a time, I recall my father climbing an icy ladder to the top of our house, in the dead of winter, taking with him a large coffee can and two bottles of orange soda pop. We didn't have a carrot for our snowman's nose. He punched a hole in the bottom of the metal coffee can and poured both bottles of soda in it. The orange mixture slowly dripped from the roof edge onto an ice cycle that was already formed. A couple hours later, we had an orange ice cycle. Then, my father once more climbed the slippery ladder and broke the ice cycle loose from the roof edge. He had made our snowman a very special nose.

When the sun came out the next day and the temperature rose above freezing, our snowman's nose started to drip. Father told us our snowman had a head cold and a runny nose. My brothers and I felt sorry for Frosty. We ran to the back porch of our house where the dog slept. We grabbed the old blanket that the dog slept on. We ran back around the house, with our dog chasing us, and wrapped our snowman in it to comfort him.

CHAPTER ELEVEN

Depression Day Doll Furniture

I was born during World War II. There were ration cards and some things were hard to come by. My mother stood in a line, a block long, to buy one pound of bacon. Needless to say, toys were not priority items.

I received a doll once a year on Christmas and perhaps a book of paper dolls on my birthday. Doll furniture wasn't a priority with my parents, who were struggling to keep food on the table. The country's poor were trying to overcome the Great Depression. My father was wearing cardboard in his shoes at that time because there was no money for shoes. Food and shelter were the first priorities.

Mothers back then were innovative. Doll furniture was made for little girls and was not always done to one inch scale as it is today. You might have all sizes mixed together. Tuna can chairs were popular as well as bathtubs made from Sardine cans. Salt boxes were cut down and made into rocking cradles. Jelly jar lids became doll dishes. Worn out pot holders became area rugs. Mothers used what they had and made temporary toys to pacify their little girls who were begging for doll furniture.

I was luckier than my friends. I had a kitchen cabinet with a sink in it. My treasure was a Hershey cocoa tin with the little shiny metal round disc on the top for my sink. Imagination made it the greatest kitchen cabinet ever.

Life was good, even if we were short on purchased material items. My mother wore an apron every time she cooked. When it came time for meals, my mother sat at one end in our tiny kitchen and my father at the other end. We six kids stood three to each side of the table. Our parents didn't own chairs for us. However, even though we were suffering from the effects of the depression and World War II, we ate at regular times and grace was always said. Did I mention that my mother did not have dessert plates or bowls? She barely had a plate a piece for us to eat off of and one pan to cook in. When we had dessert, usually cake, we turned our plate upside down and the clean underside of it became our dessert plate. I literally have eaten upside down cake and stood up to eat it.

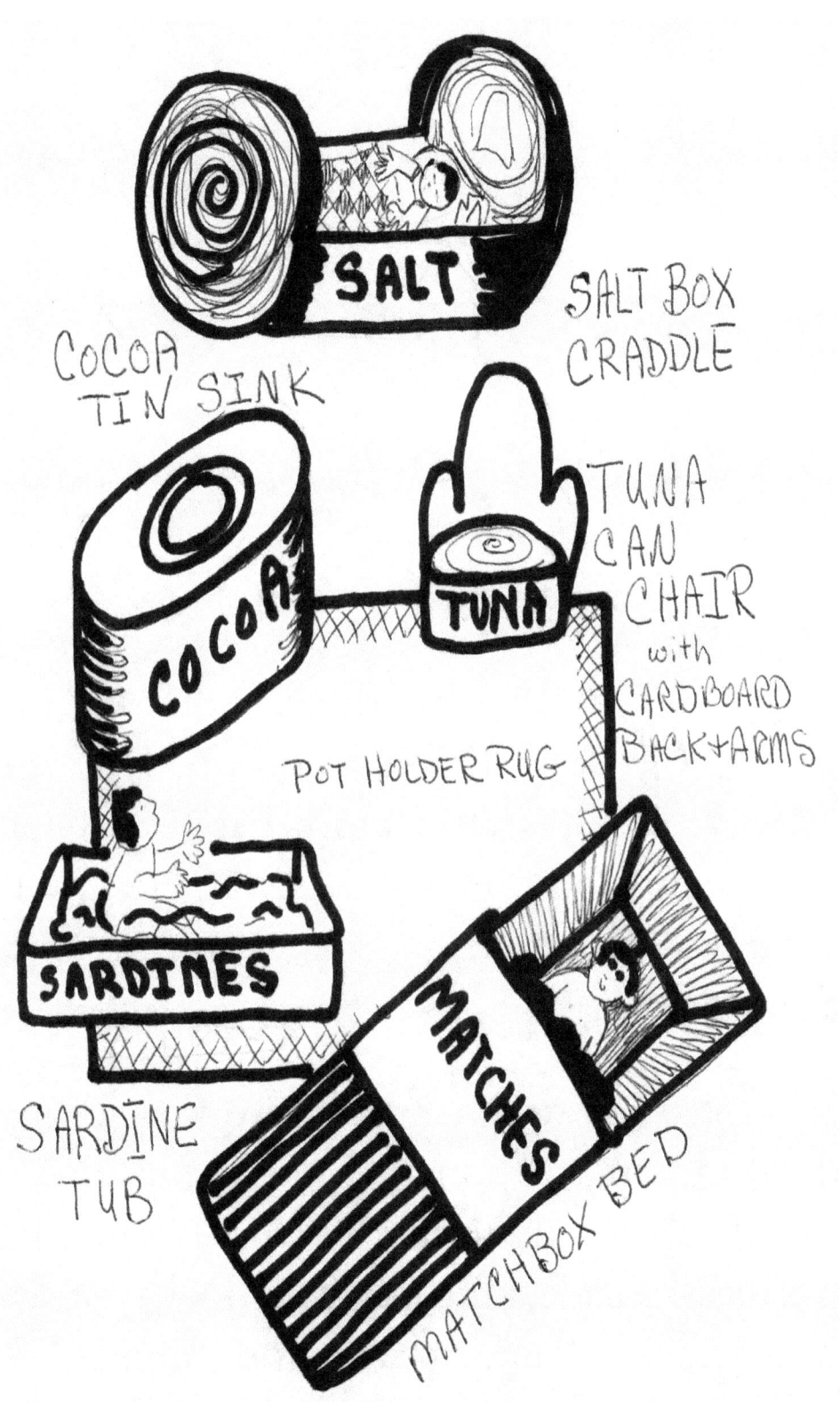

COCOA TIN SINK

SALT BOX CRADDLE

TUNA CAN CHAIR with CARDBOARD BACK+ARMS

POT HOLDER RUG

SARDINE TUB

MATCHBOX BED

CHAPTER TWELVE

"I dropped my Dolly in the Dirt"

By Jo Hammers

My name is Molly and I am the dolly that got dropped in the dirt. How did it happen? That terrible little boy, Jeffrey caused it. He frightened Jodie, the little girl who owns me, with a snake.

Her mother told her afterward that Jeffrey did odd things like that because he liked her. I say he does odd things like that because he is a mean, crude, little boy who doesn't know what the word 'like' means. Jodie agrees.

This is my take on the event.

I was skipping rope with Jodie, the little girl who owns me. We were having a wonderful time. As she skipped the rope with me in her arms, my curly hair would bounce up and down with the movement. This was a good thing. Jodie had washed my hair earlier and the movement up and down was drying it. There were no hair dryers in the days when I belonged to Jodie. You towel dried your hair and then let Mother Nature do the rest.

We were having a wonderful time when out of nowhere Jeffrey, the boy who did odd things, appeared carrying a live garden snake. He walked right up to our faces and shook the live, hissing snake at Jodie. It was not a poisonous snake, but Jodie did not know that. She jumped back in horror with me in her arms. She then tried to put some distance between her and Jeffrey. In doing so, she stepped back into a muddy hole.

Jeffrey didn't take the hint that she was not into snakes. He walked toward her and shook it in our faces again. Jodie was so frightened that she let go of me and I fell landing in the mud hole. Then Jodie ran like crazy. Jodie had dropped me, her dolly, in the dirt. I was not happy about it. My freshly washed hair fell into muddy water and my clean doll dress was soiled. Even worse, I couldn't get up. Dolls don't get up unless their little girl owner's want them to.

I was disgusted.

Lying quietly in the mud hole, I watched the disgusting little boy chase her across the playground, shaking the curling snake at her. Jodie yelled, screeched, and ran every which direction trying to get away from him. I lay in the dirt watching the whole situation. I had dirt on my clothes, on my skin, and in my hair. I shivered thinking about it.

Finally, Jeffrey tripped and fell. The snake got away from him and quickly slithered off into the tall grass. He suddenly started crying. The fall had skinned his knee. I didn't feel sorry for him. He didn't feel sorry for me lying in the mud hole. However, I am not as nice of a person as the little girl who owns me. Seeing he was hurt, she returned and helped him to his feet and home to his mother.

Where was I during her escorting of him home? My little girl not only dropped me in the dirt, she left me there. I am thinking about trading her in for a new owner. I hear there are charity bins where dolls like me get new homes.

I laid in the dirt for at least an hour before she returned for me.

"Are you hurt?" Jodie asked picking me up.

"No!" I answered.

I really wasn't hurt, just soiled. However, no frilly, prissy doll wants to be seen dirt covered; much less have their hair washed a second time in one day.

BAD BOY JEFFREY

~ *A Poem*

Run, girlie, run

Because it is time

To have some fun!

Here I come chasing

You with my pet snake

To hear you scream.

I am one mean

Boy mischief machine.

You better run

And not hesitate.

I will get you with my snake

And then laugh

When you cry and screech.

My name is Jeffrey and

I am a peach.

CHAPTER THIRTEEN

The Gypsy Doll

My friend Judy had a dream. When she grew up, she was going to run away with a circus and become its gypsy fortune teller. If she got a new doll, she immediately undressed it and wrapped its head and body with scraps of fabric, turning it into a gypsy. She would make necklaces and jewelry for her gypsies out of macaroni and make them crystal balls out of marbles. She was obsessed.

I am not quite sure where her passion for gypsies came from. Her mom was single and

worked as a waitress. Her father, she

saw once a year at Christmas for possibly an hour. Both of her parents were from Native American descent and from Oklahoma. The circus did come to our city once a year. However, I don't remember them having a fortune teller. To this day, I do not know what her passion for gypsies was all about.

Now, every time I run across a gypsy doll, I immediately think of her and the many hours we played together when we were children.

As a child, I dreamed of living in a southern mansion with white pillars out front. I saw myself throwing Southern, elegant, dinner parties and my daughter's room filled with china dolls.

Now, it is sixty years later. My friend became a florist after high school and then a landlord who now owns a full city block of houses, both sides of the street. Whether or not she tells fortunes or reads the crystal ball for her tenants, I do not know. Perhaps she is one lucky little secret gypsy. She always knew she was going to be someone when she was a child. She always had dreams.

I have never lived in a southern mansion but have basically become a hermit instead. I don't give large dinner parties. I prefer to eat in restaurants and entertain my family and friends that way. I do have a daughter and she loved cabbage patch dolls, not china headed ones. Am I a success? Definitely yes! I found an easier way to entertain with no clean up or maid to pay. I live a simple life in a cabin in the Ozark Mountains with my memories, dolls from my youth, and my books. I am a writer. So is my daughter. She has currently written seven books. I have written eighteen.

Just as my friend Judy and I were different as children, we are different in our adult successes. I was a dreamer during the Great Depression, so was Judy. Our dreams and fantasies kept us focused on improved futures for ourselves. We, as humans, have free will choice. We must choose good lives and pursue them. Children should be encouraged to dream and choose bigger and better. Wise parents point their children in the upward direction to follow their dreams.

GYPSY DOLL

~ *A Poem*

MIRROR, MIRROR ON THE WALL

Mirror, mirror on the wall

Who is the fairest doll of all?

Of course, you have to say me!

Mirror, mirror on the wall

Who is the vainest doll of all?

Of course . . . me . . . me . . . me!

PALMS READ

GYPSY

TEA LEAVES READ

The Gypsy Doll

My parents lived one city block off the railroad tracks. In the 1940s and 50s it wasn't uncommon for a hobo to knock on our back door and ask for food. We had a tree stump out back that stood up about two feet in the air after being cut down. That is where my parents fed those wandering along, if they had anything to share. My parents had chickens back then. Usually what my parents gave the strangers were a couple of fried eggs and a piece of bread. Some people in the depression didn't even have the eggs. Monday thru Saturday at my house we ate either beans and cornbread or biscuits and gravy for dinner. Once a week we had fried chicken and dessert. For breakfast, like most kids back then, we had oatmeal and a slice of bread. Milk was not drunk. The gallon of milk, purchased for the week, was saved for cooking and the making of gravy. Until times got better in the early 1950s, I don't ever recall anything but water served at our table. Once a year, my father would dig sassafras and my mother would make tea out of it. Now, that was some nasty stuff. I stuck with the water. A can of coffee was kept to make for my father who carried a lunch box and a thermos to work. There was no fast food to speak of back then. Weekend picnics were popular. Today, kids think an outing is a visit to a fast food place. We had picnics where we made sandwiches with just butter and sugar on them. Perhaps the sugar wasn't so good for our teeth, but it was what we had. The poor, coming out of the Great Depression, survived and made memories with what they had. Picnicking in the park and eating butter sandwiches was a good thing. It was quality time spent with my parents.

My mother cooked everything from scratch.

Her specialties were chicken and dumplings (she had to wring the chicken's neck), banana cake, and biscuits to die for. Life was simple and the food was simple. People sat on their lawns at night and talked with the neighbors. There were no televisions in our neighborhood at that time. I have fond memories of chasing fireflies with the neighbor kids and playing like we were a marching band. Each kid made their own instrument noise. There were no actual instruments.

Window shopping was a popular past time in the forties and early fifties. Couples would go downtown and just look in shop windows late in the evening just before sun down after the businesses had closed for the day. It was entertainment that didn't cost anything. I recall standing in front of a five and ten store window looking at a small, elegantly dressed, lady doll with a big skirt that was stuffed like a cushion. She had no legs. I recall her arms holding numerous little items and she had a piece of fabric wrapped around her tiny head like she was a gypsy. I remember looking at a tiny hand mirror sewed on to her skirt. Now, I realize she was a pin cushion doll. Women back then kept them on their dressers to stick hat pins in. My aunt had one dressed in 4th of July costume.

PIN CUSHION DOLL

I recall telling my friend all about her, when I got home from shopping with my parents. My friend was into gypsy dolls and was all ears. Her mother went back to the store and purchased the special Gypsy lady. My friend had the only mother in the neighborhood that worked. Her working mother doted on her and bought her things the rest of us could only dream about.

When we were grown, this friend told me that the one thing her mother could not buy her was the smell of yeast bread baking and a mother and dad who were always present at meals. Her mother was a divorcee who didn't get home till seven in the evening. She worked long hours to provide what she thought was a good life for her and my friend. My friend wanted a mother and a father sitting at the dinner table and a mother who baked bread. Instead, she had a Gypsy doll and things. I had what she truly wanted. She wanted a family.

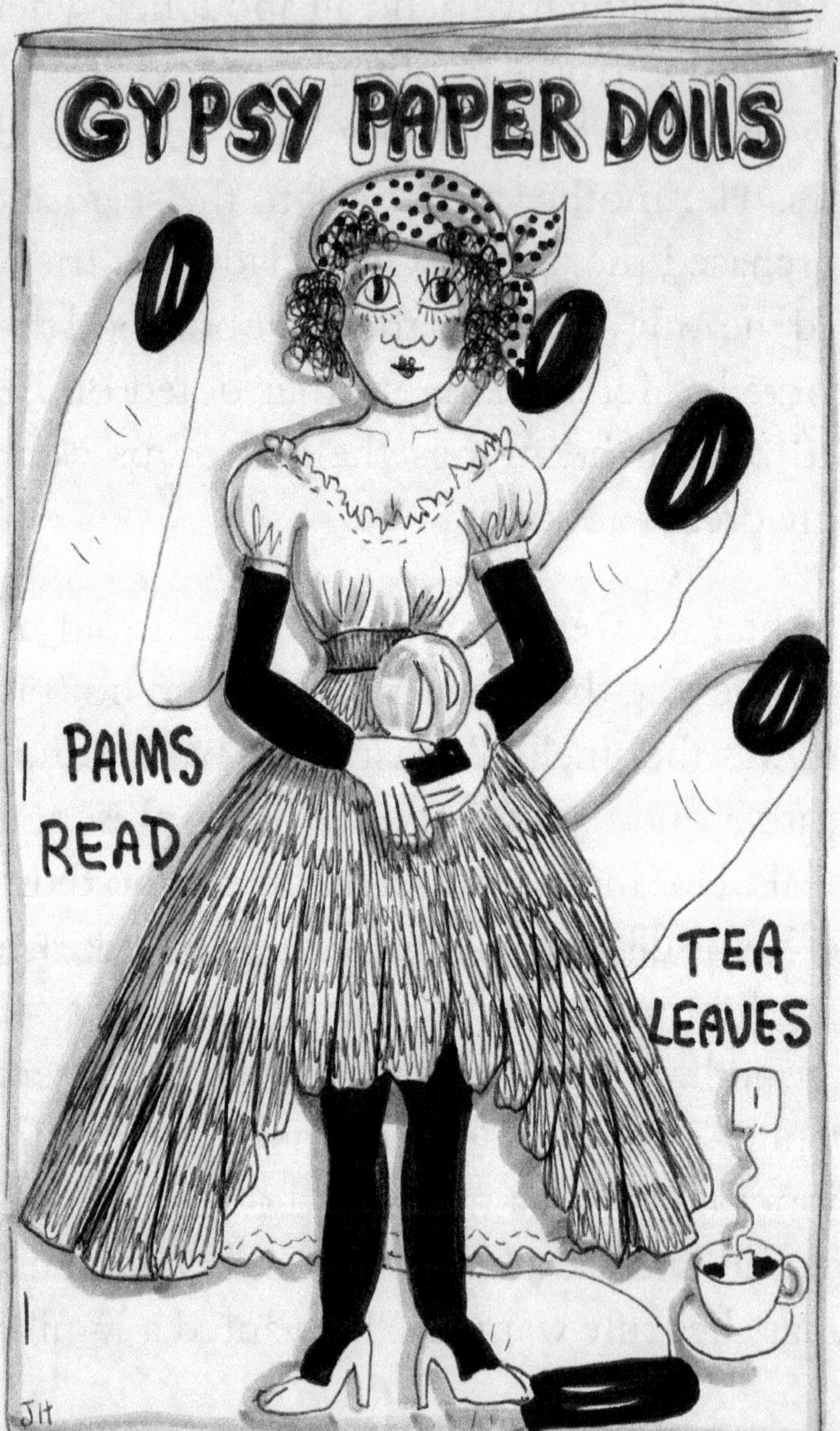
GYPSY PAPER DOLLS
PALMS READ
TEA LEAVES
JH

GYPSY Doll . . . GYPSY Doll

~ *A Poem*

"Gypsy Doll, Gypsy Doll tell me please

What in your doll mirror do you see?"

In the looking glass I now see,

A Gypsy mind reader looking back at me!

In the misty eyes of others I see,

Love I have given returning to me.

In the cloudy past I see,

The arms of a child adoring me!

In the future I look and see

a crystal ball to eye

and palms to read.

Gypsy Doll . . . Gypsy Doll, I agree.

Your mirror has spoken truthfully."

CHAPTER FOURTEEN

The Paper Doll Club

One elementary school year, my teacher showed us girl students how to cut book marks from the Sunday Newspaper. We would cut long rectangle pieces out of the fashion ads. I also recall her showing us how to fold newspaper and then cut chains of dolls. She probably saw it as a frugal, low budget, art project. To me, it was a lesson in being creative that has never left me. I still cut my own book marks from discarded cardboard boxes and magazine covers.

The Sunday paper was a biggie at our house.

My parents could not afford to take the paper thru the week. They just took the Sunday paper. There were no television sets back then, so the newspaper was the weekend entertainment. I had to wait till my parents were completely thru reading the paper before I could cut out the pretty fashion ladies and make paper dolls out of them. After cutting them out, I would lay them on my Big Chief writing tablet and draw around them to make clothes.

I had two friends during that time. We all made newspaper fashion lady paper dolls. One summer, we formed a paper doll club. To be a member you had to draw paper dolls. We met on Mondays in one of our backyards to show off and exchange dolls we had made on Sunday. I preferred drawing ladies in hi-heels and pretty dresses. My friend Judy drew gypsies. My other friend drew bears, cats, dogs, and ladies in bathing suits. I am sure that each of us thought that our creations were the best.

Like any childhood play, sometimes you do things your parents are not too happy about. One of my two friends drew a lady paper doll and then painted its bathing suit on with her mother's red nail polish. The thought was very creative. However, her mother did not see it that way. My friend had laid the paper lady on her mother's wooden table without paper under it. Then she painted the doll and the table with the polish. That ended our paper doll club. Her angry mother forbade her to cut or make anymore dolls.

A few years back, I got the nicest hand-made Christmas card from my old friend. She had drawn a paper doll on it and painted its clothes with fingernail polish. The card read: Merry Christmas – Remember When? P. S. I put paper down before painting this card on my mother's table which I just inherited.

SUMMER SALLY

SUMMER SALLY - Bonju 1997

SUMMER SALLY

~ *A Poem*

The rich dolls live up the street.

I am Summer Sally who lives down the alley.

A little girl purchased me for ninety-nine cents.

I belong to a child who was Heaven sent.

The rich dolls up the street sit on shelves and are lonely.

Everywhere my little girl goes, she takes me with her.

My little girl's Mother, Aunts, and Grannies

Sew and make me fancy hats and dresses.

They make me pajamas and bows for my tresses.

I gladly twist, turn, dance and bow wearing

My designer clothes made by those who know how to sew.

I may not be rich like the dolls up the street

But I don't sit on a shelf all day and weep.

I have a family that loves plain old ninety-nine cent me.

My name is Sally and I live down the alley.

I am one very lucky ninety-nine cent poor child's doll.

I am not a forgotten flower on a wall.

THE END

www.ingramcontent.com/pod-product-compliance
Lightning Source LLC
Chambersburg PA
CBHW071339130626
46556CB00004B/1948